THE *Wounded* BUTTERFLY

Francis Mann
Illustrated by Martin Piwowarski

Published by BookLocker.com, Inc., Trenton, Georgia.

Printed on acid-free paper.

First printing edition 2022.

ISBN: 979-8-88531-059-8 Hardcover
ISBN: 979-8-88531-147-2 Paperback

Dedicated to my feline companions who wait for me in God's heavenly home: my beloved Newman, Pokey, Francis and Elegant Lady. To Prince—my family's beloved Golden Retriever. To Cricket, my beloved Severe Macaw, and to my beloved, feisty African Grey Parrot, Pepper.

To my beloved feline companions still here with me:
Martin, Momma, Ebony (aka the Wicked Witch) and Smokey.

To my beloved late parents Helen and Frank.
To my late brothers Jeffrey and Jude Michael.
To my beloved late Grandfather Joseph Hirtz.

This book is likewise dedicated to a champion for life who helped make this book possible—Don Magnotta.

Once upon a time there was a tenderhearted boy, a happy little lad named Billy.

Billy loved to play in the garden by his house, where he always found much joy and laughter. This magical place was home to all God's creatures—even a family of mischievous little mice!

Here rows and rows of rainbow-colored flowers
seemed to dance around the tall, handsome trees.

Bluebirds and sparrows spent fun-filled hours gliding through the bright open sky, swooping to smile at the busy, buzzy bumble bees.

In the garden many critters lived happily in every nook and cranny. They were of every size and shape and came from every age and place.

Little Billy made many special friends —so many kind and caring friends. Day after day, there was always love and friendship in the garden by the house.

One bright, sunny day, Billy watched a frizzy, fuzzy caterpillar tip-toe up a tree.

She crept and crawled, stretched and sprawled—slinking up, then slithering down the proud and happy tree.

"Little caterpillar, will you please stay and play with me?" Billy asked. He listened to the caterpillar's tiny whisper as she said,

"I promise to stay and I would like to play.
Please pick me up gently, so gently I pray.
Yes, we shall be happy together today,
And perhaps in your garden is where I will stay."

Day after day, Billy and the caterpillar stayed and played.
They became good friends—very good friends indeed.

Billy watched as his friend climbed to the top of a tree,
as if she were reaching for the stars.

The caterpillar watched as Billy lay in the grass,
cherishing the beauty of nature that cradled him.

But one rainy day in May, something wasn't quite right.

"Little caterpillar," cried Billy, "why are you not moving?"

The caterpillar did not answer.

She did not move at all.

Billy waited patiently to play with his friend.

But she still would not move, not an itty bit.

"This is very strange, very strange indeed," said Billy.

Then something quite unusual happened…

"Look! The caterpillar is wrapping herself in a warm, wooly blanket!" Billy exclaimed.

Soon the teensy body was tightly tucked
away inside a snuggly cocoon!

"What has happened? Where did my little
friend go?" Billy sadly asked.

The flowers and the trees were silent,
although they knew the answer.

"She told me she would stay. She promised she
would play. She knows I love her so!"

The caterpillar slept.

Time went by so slowly as she silently slept.
Day after day, night after night, she slept...

The clock went tick-tock,
tock-tick,
tickety-tock,
yet still the caterpillar slept.

She slept by day, she slept by night…
Tockity-tick, she slept around the clock.

Then one day…it happened…

Billy gazed at something special—very special indeed!

"Look!" He could hardly believe his eyes. "The caterpillar changed. She really did change! How did this happen?"

"She's a butterfly!" Billy shouted again and again, "a beautiful butterfly—as red as the reddest roses in the garden!

This beautiful creature with angel's wings,
glowed bright with eternal love.

Now Billy Boy knew, down deep in his heart,
she was sent from heaven above!

Day after day, Billy and the butterfly played in the garden.

Then, on yet another rainy morning, Billy's little friend seemed so very sick—and oh, so very sad.

"Look! Look!" Billy shouted again and again." Her wing is badly broken and now she cannot fly!"

"Little baby butterfly, how did you get hurt?" Billy sweetly asked.

Once again, the flowers and the trees listened. They had no answer.

Billy held the butterfly close to his heart. He kissed his precious friend ever so softly, all the while seeking a blessing from above.

Tiny teardrops fell from Billy's eyes. He felt as if his heart would break from sorrow as he heard his fragile friend sigh.

Silently, Billy's tears touched the wounded wing.
He found words deep in his soul as he sang to her:

"Please, my baby butterfly,
Please, oh please, don't go.
You are my friend. I love you…
more than you will ever know!"

Night after night, day in and day out, Billy held the butterfly close to his heart.
He gave her his precious love, as that was all he had to give.

Then, one misty, moonlit night, Billy lay sound asleep. He dreamed pleasant
dreams of the cherished friendship he shared with his wounded friend.

Suddenly, the butterfly lifted her head, spread her wings
and flew to the open window. Softly she whispered…

"Thank you, my sweet, gentle boy,
Thank you my one treasured friend.
Your warmth and love, your giving heart,
have helped my wing to mend!"

Early the next morning, Billy went to the garden to pray,
a place he felt so safe and blessed.

There he fed some feathered friends and smiled
as he watched them cuddle in their cozy nest.

Suddenly, as Billy looked up at the vast, open sky, he saw her! A playful little teardrop twinkled in the corner of his eye, as he softly sang,

"You are my wondrous butterfly,
I watch you soar up to the sky.
You look so well, you rise so high.
My love for you will never die!"

The butterfly swooped down and embraced her dear friend. She kissed his round, rosy cheek, replacing all the doubt and fear with friendship and love.

Then the butterfly whispered to Billy her promise everlasting, one that she would never break:

"I will love you forever my dear Billy Boy,
even if someday we part.
Now and for always, as God's special child,
you will forever remain in my heart."

"The vocation of being a 'protector' is not just something involving Christians alone; it also has a prior dimension which is simply human, involving everyone.

It means protecting all creation, the beauty of the created world, as the Book of Genesis tells us and as Saint Francis of Assisi showed us. It means respecting each of God's creatures and respecting the environment in which we live."

— Pope Francis